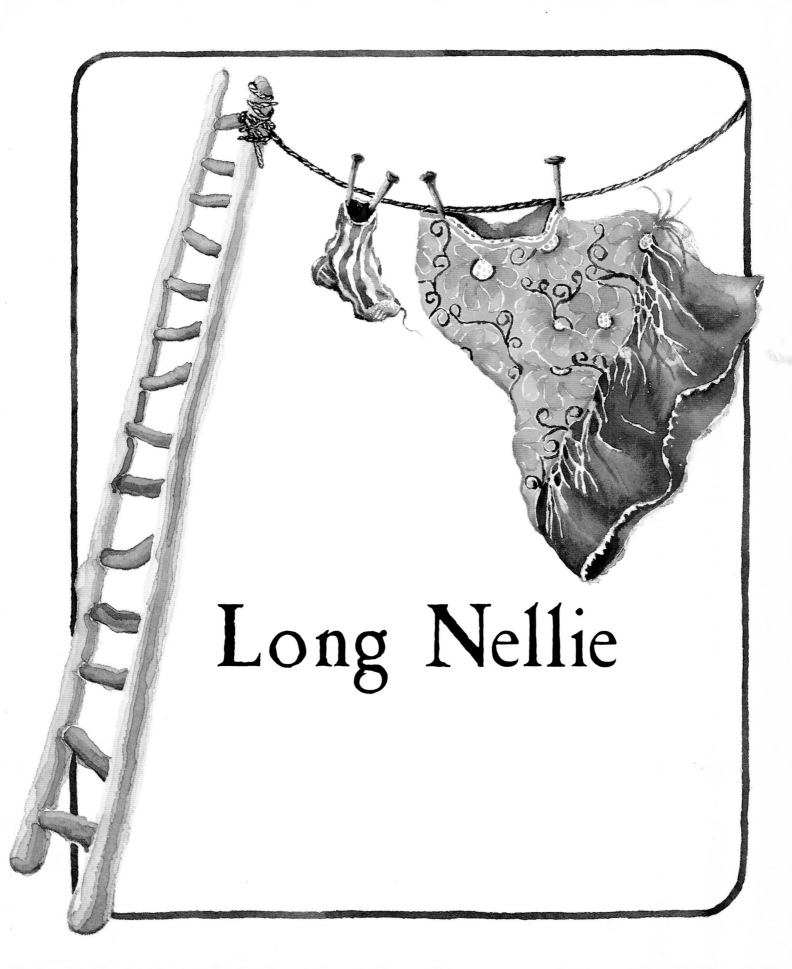

Long Nellie

For my gypsy parents, Gene and Shirley, who raised me on the outskirts
D.T.-Z.

Long Nellie

Deborah Turney-Zagwÿn

Orca Book Publishers

EVERY morning Long Nellie gathered sticks on the outskirts of the village. There, treelimbs were unpinned by the wind. She collected these castoffs to fill her woodstove.

Long Nellie was as thin as a curved rake and as tall as a bent stepladder. Gathering firewood, she looked like the stem of a wild leafless tree.

Long Nellie lived in a scarlet trailer. She would shake off her wooden bundle near the doorstep, except for her pocket twigs, which she carried inside to light her fire with.

Gray smoke curled up kinked pipe, smudging the sky above. Below, cloudier than smoke, plastic veiled the windows of the caravan. Neighbours couldn't see in. Long Nellie couldn't see out.

Jeremy's mom told him that Long Nellie was a scavenger. "She picks up what others throw away. No one thanks her for it. It's a pretty lonely occupation."

In Jeremy's family, they threw away very little. Food scraps were shaken into a slatted box by the garden. Newspapers, jars and cans were tied, washed and flattened for a recycling container at the edge of the neighbourhood. Their garbage can was usually empty.

"There is nothing in there Long Nellie would want," Jeremy told his mom. She nodded. It was true.

One morning Jeremy's bike developed an annoying squeak. A tad of elbow grease and a tin of axle grease would squelch that squeak. Elbow grease they had lots of, but the axle grease had hidden its oily self somewhere in the garage. Jeremy's dad hunted high while Jeremy looked low. In the middle of their search, a whining sound crept, faint but insistent, through the garage window.

Jeremy's dad leaned over the sill and lifted the lid of the garbage can. Two yellow marbles winked below.

"Maybe it's a rat, Dad." Jeremy hung over the can for a closer look. Two yellow eyes blinked...wide and frightened.

A pink mouth with
sharp teeth hissed . . .
broken whiskers framed
a grimy nose.

Gingerly Jeremy
reached down and pulled
the wriggling bundle out
of the can. It was no rat!

It was a very little,
scruffy cat. Jeremy's dad
sneezed. The boy
wrapped the kitten with
its bitey teeth and
scratchy claws,
squirming, in a slightly
soiled grease rag.

"Seems hungry, Dad."
Jeremy's dad sneezed a
string of sneezes.

In the kitchen Jeremy let the cat twist free, flopping out of its wrappings into a saucer of milk. The sound brought his mom into the room.

"Bad table manners," was her first comment. "Awful skinny, probably has worms," she added.

The kitten flipped itself sideways to scratch its ear, then scoured the dish clean.

"Fleas too!" his mom shook her head. "Sorry Son. Cat hair in the air makes your dad's nose drip like a faucet. We'll have to find a home for this orphan. Can you think of anyone?"

Jeremy glanced up at his dad keeping his distance, then down at the kitten...homely and homeless. Not his to keep. This kitten reminded him of someone...skinny, scruffy, alone. Long Nellie! What if he arranged for the two of them to meet?

His mom wasn't sure about this idea. "We don't know Long Nellie that well. She seems lonely, but that doesn't mean she'd welcome an orphan. Long Nellie is a bit of a gypsy you know. She wanders, without any ties."

Jeremy thought of Long Nellie's trailer with its old tarp, weighed down with rocks and wheel hubs. He thought of her unsmiling face. Even gypsies needed company. "What is the use of gathering sticks for a fire," he told his mom, "if there is no one to share it with?"

She nodded. It was true.

Jeremy knew that Long Nellie would be making her trip to the neighbourhood dumpster soon. Once a week, Long Nellie, as tall as a bent stepladder, would clamber up the huge bin and kneel on its upper ledge. He had seen her bony hands lift out bottles and cans — once, a sweater with a hole in the elbow.

Today Jeremy planned for Long Nellie to find a lively little treasure... would she take it home?

The kitten was well fed and drowsy. Jeremy made it a cozy nest in his old fishing basket, wrapping the worn straps around the handlebars of his bike. He heard a halfhearted hiss as they bumped down the gravelled driveway, but later the rocking movement of the fishbasket over smooth pavement must have lulled the kitten to sleep.

Jeremy knew he didn't have much time. Long Nellie would already be plodding down the hill from her trailer, her plastic sack trailing behind her. She was never late. The full dumpster would be traded for an empty one shortly after her visit. If Jeremy got there before Long Nellie, he could leave the basket on the bin's ledge. She would find it there for sure.

Would she take it home?

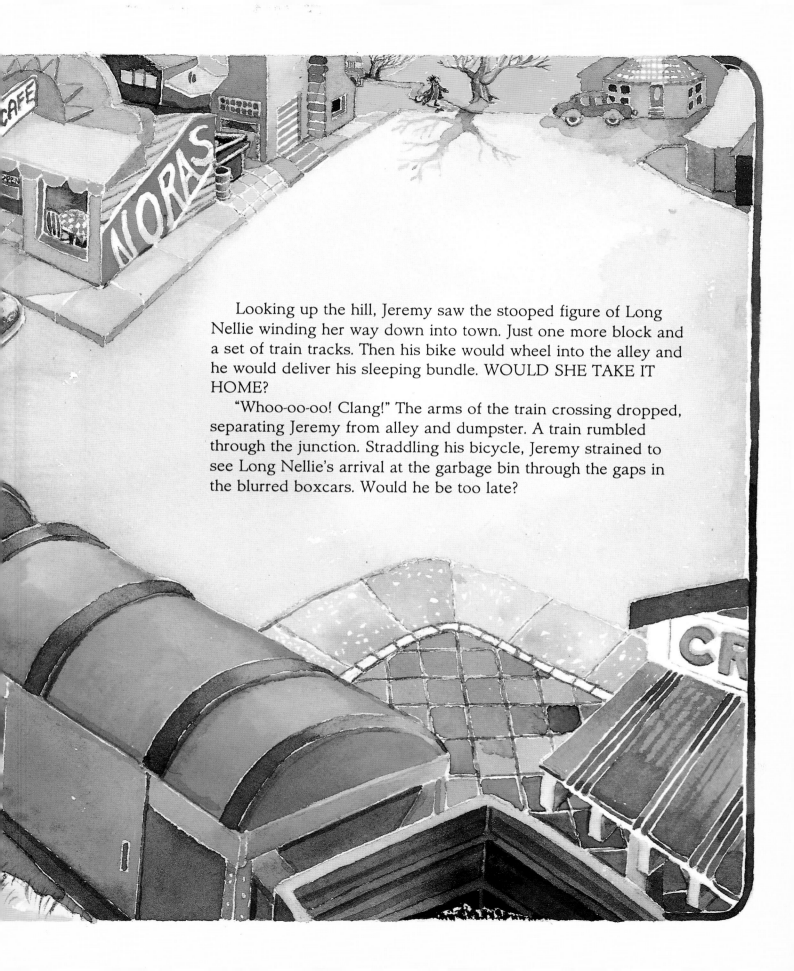

Looking up the hill, Jeremy saw the stooped figure of Long Nellie winding her way down into town. Just one more block and a set of train tracks. Then his bike would wheel into the alley and he would deliver his sleeping bundle. WOULD SHE TAKE IT HOME?

"Whoo-oo-oo! Clang!" The arms of the train crossing dropped, separating Jeremy from alley and dumpster. A train rumbled through the junction. Straddling his bicycle, Jeremy strained to see Long Nellie's arrival at the garbage bin through the gaps in the blurred boxcars. Would he be too late?

The train passed. Inside the wicker basket, the kitten stretched but didn't waken. The crossing-arms flipped upwards. Jeremy slid onto the pedals of his bike and whirled over the tracks into the alley on the other side. He braked behind the dumpster and swung the basket up to the ledge in front...easy to see, impossible to overlook. Still that kitten slept.

Had Long Nellie come and gone?

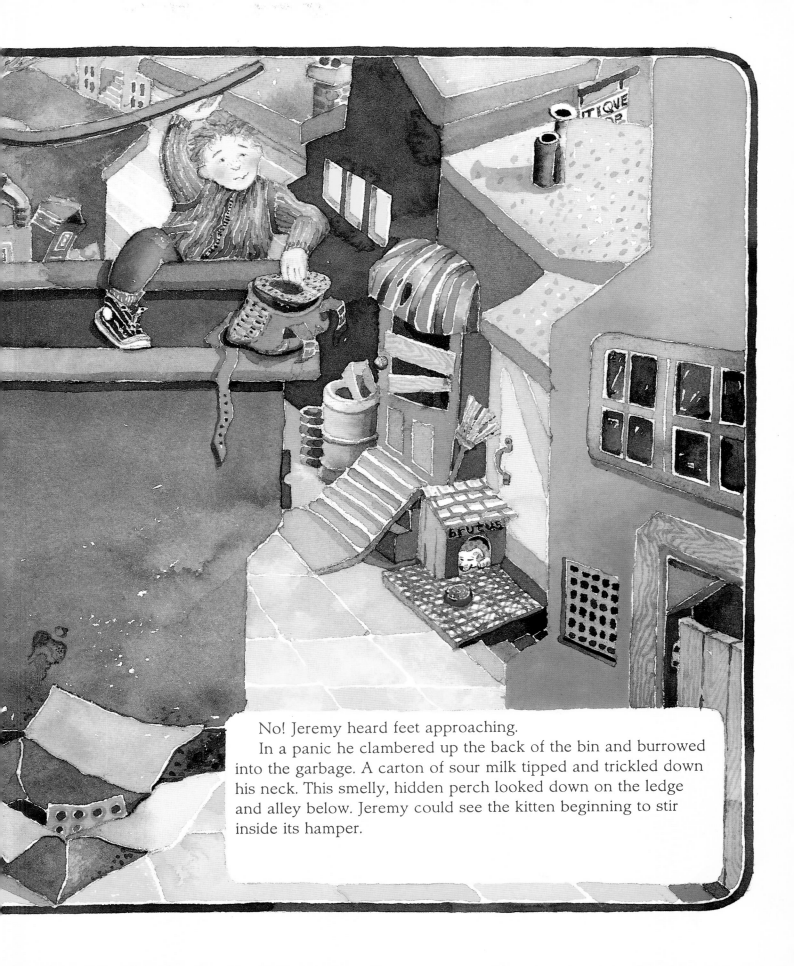

No! Jeremy heard feet approaching.

In a panic he clambered up the back of the bin and burrowed into the garbage. A carton of sour milk tipped and trickled down his neck. This smelly, hidden perch looked down on the ledge and alley below. Jeremy could see the kitten beginning to stir inside its hamper.

Long Nellie was very close. Her coat was unbuttoned and her shoes were untied. Frayed laces flew behind Long Nellie's feet as she hurried towards the dumpster and the kitten's ledge. Jeremy could see a pair of drowsy eyes watching from under the fishbasket's flap. Would Long Nellie take this kitten home?

In front of the bin Long Nellie paused. She fingered the flap of the wicker basket. She stood on her tiptoes to squint at it. An empty fishbasket would suit her fine. But no rush. She wanted to check out the bin first before she bagged the basket.

Nellie circled the dumpster. She discovered Jeremy's bike and leapt up into a one-legged wobbly position on its seat. Flinging her free leg upwards, Nellie heaved herself, swaying, onto the ledge.

Face to face with wide-eyed Jeremy!

Then two things happened. The little cat shrieked and leapt out of the basket. Nellie screeched and fell head first into the garbage bin.

"Don't worry!" Jeremy told Nellie's feet. He flicked a stale noodle off his forehead. "I'll rescue you!"

Long Nellie was having difficulty turning herself rightside up. One unlaced foot had twisted. Her other foot was flapping furiously — upside down froglike!

Jeremy hoisted Nellie upright. He brushed the coffee grounds off her collar. Coaxing the kitten from the ledge, Jeremy slipped it into his pocket where the smell of sour milk and tinned tuna lingered. The little cat liked that.

Nellie leaned on Jeremy. They hobbled to the outskirts where Jeremy propped his bike against a tree and helped Long Nellie climb the slope to her trailer. Long Nellie's face was close to his as they struggled up the steps and through her door. In spite of an aching foot, Long Nellie seemed almost cheerful. Hers was a worn face, a shy face, but not an uncaring face. The kitten purred in the jacket pocket between them. They both felt it.

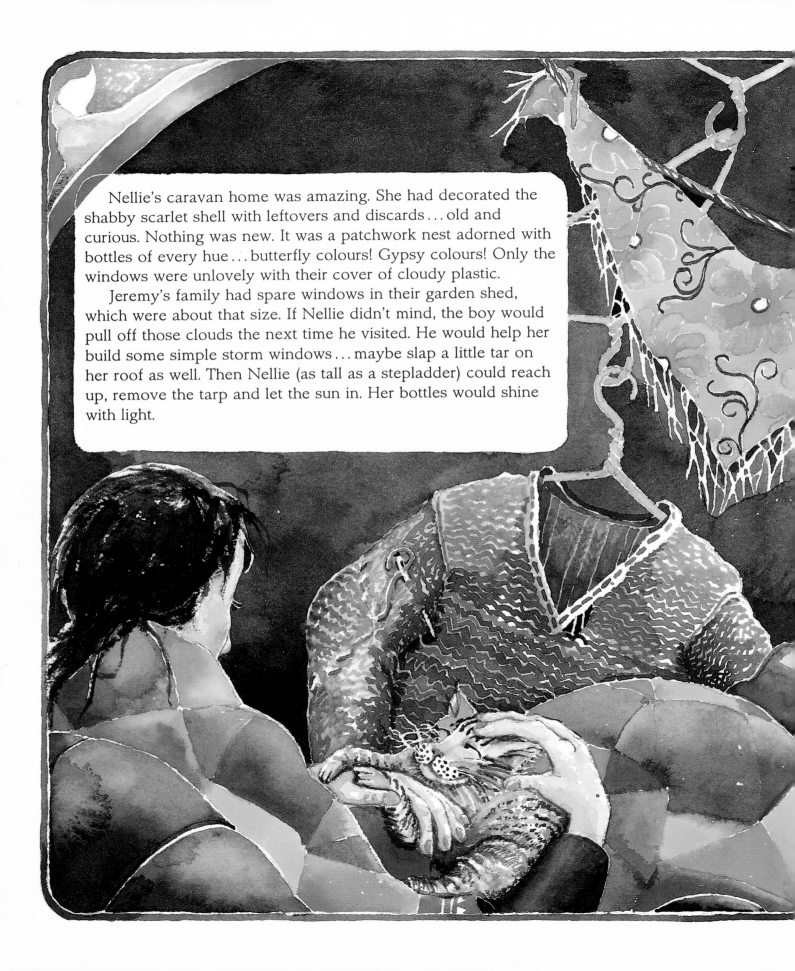

Nellie's caravan home was amazing. She had decorated the shabby scarlet shell with leftovers and discards...old and curious. Nothing was new. It was a patchwork nest adorned with bottles of every hue...butterfly colours! Gypsy colours! Only the windows were unlovely with their cover of cloudy plastic.

Jeremy's family had spare windows in their garden shed, which were about that size. If Nellie didn't mind, the boy would pull off those clouds the next time he visited. He would help her build some simple storm windows...maybe slap a little tar on her roof as well. Then Nellie (as tall as a stepladder) could reach up, remove the tarp and let the sun in. Her bottles would shine with light.

Jeremy settled Nellie in her wellworn armchair and put the kitten on her lap. He pinned her shawl and mismatched socks above the old heater to warm. He lit the fire with a handful of pocket twigs. The heater smoked, then glowed and breathed a wonderful warmth. The kitten rolled onto its back and lifted a hind paw to scratch a flea...but Long Nellie's fingers were quicker. She gave it a good rub behind the ears instead. The kitten stretched and arched, yawned and purred.

Above the heater Nellie's clothes hung...gypsy clothes... bright as the flags on a circus tent. Jeremy unpegged the toasty socks and gently pulled them up (first one, then the other) over Long Nellie's tired feet.

Then the boy made tea, poured hot from a chipped china pot.

Orca Book Publishers
PO Box 5626, Station B
Victoria, BC   V8R 6S4
Canada

Orca Book Publishers
1574 Gulf Road, Box 3028
Point Roberts, WA   98281
USA

Canadian Cataloguing in Publication Data
Zagwyn, Deborah Turney,
   Long Nellie

   ISBN 0-920501-99-0
   1. Kittens — Juvenile fiction.   I. Title.
PS8599.A42L6   jC813'.54   C93–091565-8
PZ7.Z245Lo 1993

Printed and bound in Hong Kong
Design by Christine Toller & Deborah Turney-Zagwÿn